WHAT TIME IS IT, DRACULA?

Victor G. Ambrus

CROWN PUBLISHERS, INC. • *New York*

Dracula has to go to the dentist at three o'clock tomorrow. But first he has to learn to tell time. Can you help him?

Dracula wakes up. What time is it?

Dracula's friends wake up.
What time is it?

Nora Rock cooks the lunch.
What time is it?

Dracula eats his lunch.
What time is it?

Dracula goes for a walk in the forest.
What time is it?

Dracula takes the dogs for a run.
What time is it?

Dracula goes out to frighten people.
What time is it?

Dracula has a big party.
What time is it?

"It's a full moon tonight," says Mr. Werewolf.
What time is it?

It's very late, and Dracula goes to bed.
What time is it?

Now Dracula will know when it is time to go to the dentist.

Published in the United States of America by Crown Publishers, Inc.,
a Random House company, 225 Park Avenue South,
New York, New York 10003

Originally published in Great Britain by
Oxford University Press in 1991.
under the title *What's the Time, Dracula?*
CROWN is a trademark of Crown Publishers, Inc.
Manufactured in the United States of America
Library of Congress Cataloging-in-Publication Data
Ambrus, Victor G.
[What's the time, Dracula?]
What time is it, Dracula / Victor G. Ambrus
p.   cm.
Previously published as: What's the time, Dracula?
Summary: Readers must help Dracula tell time
throughout the day so that he doesn't miss
his appointment with the dentist.
[1. Time—Fiction   2. Dracula, Count
(Fictitious character)—Fiction.]   I. Title.
PZ7.A496Wh   1992
[E]—dc20   91-41260

ISBN 0-517-58970-2
10 9 8 7 6 5 4 3 2 1
First U.S. Edition